Priscilla Gets Lost!

by Laura Roetcisoender

NEWMAN SPRINGS PUBLISHING
320 Broad Street
Red Bank, NJ 07701

First originally published by Newman Springs Publishing 2021

ISBN 978-1-64531-855-2 (Paperback)
ISBN 978-1-64531-857-6 (Hardcover)
ISBN 978-1-64531-856-9 (Digital)

Printed in the United States of America

To my parents Alice and Hielke who encouraged my creativity.

1

If Priscilla had known what would happen to her that day, she might have stayed on her window sill.

While on her way to her usual breakfast spot, the Sand Dollar espresso stand, Priscilla noticed three seagulls fighting over some food. They were on a balcony of a "building" that sat on the bay. "Looks like breakfast to me!" she said as she darted over to get in on the action.

She dove after a piece knocked to the ground below. She flew down and pecked at the piece of bread for a while. When she finally looked up and saw walls and windows around her, they didn't seem familiar at all. *Where am I?* She had just finished her thought when…

5

Tooooot! The "building" boomed with a deafening sound! "Yikes! What was that?" Priscilla quickly flew up to the rafters, her feathers fluttering in the wind. Suddenly the "building" started to move! "Oh dear, I can't look," she squawked. She quickly scrunched her eyes closed. "This is worse than a bad dream," she cried. But after several minutes of the mellow up-and-down movement, she relaxed enough to fall asleep.

Varoom! Varoom! The cars began to race their engines.

"Aaacckk!" Priscilla's eyes flew awake. This was no dream! She dashed out from the rafters and sailed over the beach, but something was definitely *wrong*! This was not HER beach! Where was her espresso stand? Where was her window sill? Priscilla suddenly realized she was LOST!

"When lost, fly to the highest tree to look for help." Priscilla remembered. She headed up a hill toward a big cedar tree, but before she made it, she heard seagulls squawking below her. "I know seagulls are very smart," she said, "maybe they can help me." She landed nearby and politely waited until they were quiet.

She knew she had to ask for help, but now that she was next to them, they seemed huge! Priscilla was so afraid, she began to tremble. "What if they think I'm stupid? What if they don't want to talk to me?" she thought to herself. Priscilla waddled a little closer. "No," she said quietly, "I must be brave. Otherwise, how will I ever find my way home?" Priscilla stepped up to the closest seagull and took a deep breath. "Uh, excuse me, I'm sorry to bother you, but I've lost my way. Can you tell me where I am and how to get back home?"

"What d'ya want?" The biggest gull glared at Priscilla.

"You're lost?" they all squawked. "Why doncha' just go back the way you came?" Then they all flew away toward the beach.

"Oh, how mean!" cried Priscilla. "That wasn't helpful at all. How will I ever get home?"

She had just about given up hope when another pigeon fluttered to the ground. He waddled over to see if she had found something to eat. After her experience with the big seagulls, Priscilla was a little afraid to speak to him. "What if he's mean too?" she thought. But she was desperate to go home, so she moved a little closer. "Excuse me, I'm lost," she blurted out. "And I don't know how to get back home. Please, can you help me? My name is Priscilla. What's yours?"

"Hi Priscilla, my name's Reggie. You're on Big Island. I've always lived here, so I don't know how to go anywhere else. I'm afraid I'm not much help. How did you get here?"

Priscilla told him the whole story and added, "If you don't know how to leave here, I may never see my home again!" She squawked as she blinked back tears.

"Wait, I've got an idea," Reggie said. "Maybe my friend Bert, can help. He's a crow who's lived on this island all his life. He seems pretty smart, and I bet he knows what you should do," Reggie offered.

"Great, let's go," said Priscilla, "and thanks for going with me. You're very kind."

13

Reggie *was* very nice, maybe they could be friends.

Reggie fluffed his feathers and mumbled, "It's nothing. Happy to help."

They zoomed back down the hill and found old Bert sunning himself on a stump near the shore.

15

"Hello Reggie my boy," Bert cawed. "Where have you been? I haven't seen you lately. And who have you brought with you?"

"Hi Bert, this is my new friend Priscilla, and she can't find her way home," Reggie explained. "Can you help her?"

"Hello Priscilla, tell me your story, and I'll see if I can help." The old crow listened carefully as Priscilla explained how she landed on a "building" that moved and tooted. And when she flew away from the "building" she found herself on what Reggie called the Big Island.

Bert's eyes got real big. "That was no building you were on," he cawed. "You must've been on that thing they call a ferry. It takes cars and people back and forth from here to some other place. Were there cars on it?"

"Oh yes, and they gave me quite a fright too!" she said. "You say it goes back and forth? What do you mean?"

"The ferry comes here pretty regularly, and every time it comes in at this dock, a bunch of cars get off." Bert stretched his wings. "But don't ask me *why* or what they do once they're here. That's a mystery!"

"Hey!" Priscilla thought for a moment. "Maybe those seagulls *weren't* making fun of me after all. Maybe they were trying to tell me something! They said, '*Go back the way you came.*' Do you think if I get back on that ferry thing, it would take me home?"

"Maybe so," replied Bert. "Why don't you give it a try and see?"

"I will and thanks for your help, Bert," Priscilla said. By now, she was ready to try just about anything!

16

Priscilla and Reggie cooed their goodbyes to Bert as they made their way over to the ferry. "Gee Reggie, I'm glad you found me. What would I have done without your help?" said Priscilla.

"Oh, you're welcome." Reggie moved closer. "Say, do you think you'd ever want to come back for a visit? I could take you to some great places to eat."

"Sure, I'd like that." Priscilla nodded at Reggie, which is pigeon "talk" meaning that she liked him. "That is, if this thing does take me home. What if it takes me somewhere I don't want to go, then what?"

Reggie replied, "Then get back on it, and you'll end up here again! We'll figure out something else, but I think you'll make it home okay." Reggie sounded very encouraging.

Priscilla waved goodbye with a tip of her wing as she glided up to the rafters of the ferry. The cars drove on, the ferry tooted, and they sailed across the bay. As the ferry pulled up to the dock near Priscilla's beach, she flew out and right past her espresso stand. "Hooray, I'm almost home," she cooed. Her window sill was a welcome sight as Priscilla came in for a landing. She fluffed her feathers and laid her beak on her chest and closed her eyes. "Phew, I made it!" she thought. "Wow, I'm excited that I can go back and forth to visit my new friends. Wait till I tell everybody here about my adventure!" Priscilla sighed. "Tomorrow, I'll tell them tomorrow." And she fell fast asleep.

About the Author

Laura Roetcisoender lives on an island in Puget Sound in Washington State. She retired from US WEST telephone company and has been directly involved with children most of her life, volunteering at Pike Place Childcare and Preschool where she read books to the children and at the Family Resource Center providing child care. Besides writing many children's stories, she has written and published a family history book. This is her first children's book to be published.

CPSIA information can be obtained
at www.ICGtesting.com
Printed in the USA
JSHW041525130521
14666JS00003B/14